The Owl Who Couldn't Give a Hoot!

DON CONROY

Artist, storyteller, wildlife expert, TV presenter –
Don's talents are very varied.
His book *Cartoon Fun* was a runaway bestseller,
and his novel *On Silent Wings*, based on owl life,
was shortlisted for the Reading Association of Ireland
Award when first published.

In this series you meet the animals of the woodlands
– and a few surprises!

OTHER BOOKS IN THIS SERIES

The Tiger Who Was a Roaring Success!

The Hedgehog's Prickly Problem!

The Bat Who Was All in a Flap!

For Sarah

The Owl Who Couldn't Give a Hoot!

DON CONROY

THE O'BRIEN PRESS
DUBLIN

This revised and redesigned edition first published 1994
by The O'Brien Press Ltd.,
20 Victoria Road, Rathgar, Dublin 6, Ireland.
First published 1992.
Copyright text and illustrations © Don Conroy

British Library Cataloguing-in-publication Data
Conroy, Don. Owl Who Couldn't Give a Hoot. - New Ed.
I. Title
823. 914 [J]

The O'Brien Press receives assistance from
The Arts Council / An Chomhairle Ealaíon.

ISBN 0-86278-370-4

10 9 8 7 6 5 4 3 2 1

Cover illustration: Don Conroy
Cover design: Neasa Ní Chianáin and Michael O'Brien
Cover separations: Lithoset, Dublin
Printing: Cox & Wyman Ltd., Reading

There was once an owl who couldn't give a hoot!

Imagine! . . .
A dog who couldn't bark!
A cat who couldn't miaow!
A pig who couldn't grunt!
A sheep who couldn't bleat!
A horse who couldn't neigh!

An owl who couldn't give a hoot!

Well, it *was* a strange
story. Let me tell you
all about it.
But first, I must introduce
myself. I'm Sammy
Squirrel. I live in the
woods near Malone's
farm. I know *everything*
that happens
around here.
Actually, some friends
call me a 'know-all'.
Sometimes they say I
open my mouth and put
my foot in it! Hmmm!
Anyway, let me get on
with the story . . .

It all happened three years ago. At the edge of our woods stood an old oak tree.

Now, this tree used to be my favourite place. It had lots of branches where I could run and jump. It had lovely white flowers in spring and, best of all, acorns in autumn. It gave us squirrels most of our food for winter. It was like our very own supermarket! And everything was free!

Many birds nested there too – robins, blue tits, thrushes and chaffinches. The tree was full of song – and food.

Then a huge storm came and it was
hit by lightning. After that, no leaves or
flowers or nuts grew on it, and the
birds went away. It was all very sad.

Then a big surprise happened. Two
beautiful snowy-white owls came to
nest in the trunk of the broken tree.

They settled in one autumn, and the next spring the hen owl laid four lovely, round white eggs in the cosy nest. Soon, four fluffy little owlets hatched out.

The youngest was born quite a bit after the others and was very small. His name was Barny.

We were all longing to see the new owl babies. There had been no owls living in our area for a very long time. All the animals in the woods gathered round the oak tree.

The baby owls peeped out of the nest. They were not able to fly yet. They had soft, fuzzy white feathers. They blinked in the sunshine. Owls, you know, hunt at night and sleep during the day. Their big eyes stared down at us.

Weeks passed and the little owls grew bigger and stronger. Soon they were ready to begin to fly. All except Barny! He was still too small.

His sister and brothers were busy flapping their wings and taking practice flights out of the oak tree. I often stood below watching their antics. Sometimes they flopped down and hit the ground with a bang!

Barny watched them too. I knew he wanted to be with them and I felt sorry for him.

One day, the owl parents decided to take the older owlets on a long trial flight. Barny was to stay quietly at home.

He sat looking out at the swallows
flying low over the
fields. He even
spotted
pheasants
walking
through the
cornfields.

He saw
me, too,
looking up
at him in
his nest.
We
waved
to each
other.

Later, I decided to climb up and chat to him.

Up the tree I went, slowly in case I might frighten him. I peeped in the hole where the nest was, and there was Barny, at the back of the nest, practising flapping his wings.

He wasn't doing too well either, I thought. It would be a long time before *he* would fly!

'Hello!' I said.

Well, he gave such a shriek that I nearly fell off the tree. 'Oh, you scared me!' he said, shaking with fright.

'*I* scared *you*? What about that shriek you just gave? I almost fell!'

'But you shouldn't have sneaked up on me,' he said.

He had stopped shaking by now. We sort of knew each other, after all.

'I'm Barny.'

'I'm Sammy.'

'What kind of bird are you?' Barny asked.

'I'm not a *bird*, I'm a squirrel.'

'Can you fly?' he asked.

'No, but I can climb really quickly, and hop from tree to tree. I can *almost* fly,' I said. I did a few quick jumps and runs to show him.

'I can *almost* fly too,' Barny said, a little sadly, and he did a few flaps. 'They've all gone off today but I'm too young.'

I was about to say how sorry I was he had to stay behind when we heard a very strange noise. A very *loud* strange noise.

I hopped inside the hole and the two of us looked out. It was two men with some kind of machine.

Now, I've seen lots of machines on Malone's farm. But never one like this.

'Hold it steady, Tom,' said one man. 'Hit by lightning this tree was. Good for nothing now only firewood.'

The whole tree shook. And Barny and I shook with it. We were shaking from fright too, I can tell you.

Barny gave another piercing shriek.

The machine stopped.

'What was that?' said one man.

'It sounded weird,' said the other.

'You don't suppose the tree is haunted?'

'Don't be silly. But I must admit I never heard anything like it.'

'Oh well,' said the first man, 'let's get on with the job. We'll just cut the tree down for now and come back tomorrow and chop it up.'

The noise got louder and louder. Then the tree crashed to the ground – with us in it!

I don't know what happened after that. I woke up seeing stars – and it wasn't even night! Then I saw two of everything – two trees lying on the ground, two Barnys lying on the ground . . .

'Barny!' I shouted. There he was, flat out on the grass. I rushed over to him. For a moment I thought . . . well, I thought . . . then he suddenly sat up.

'What happened? Why are there two of you?' he asked.

'There aren't,' I said. 'Unfortunately,' I added, trying to be funny.

He didn't laugh.

'You're just dizzy after the fall,' I told him. 'Don't you remember? They cut down your tree.'

Barny gaped at the tree on the grass.

'Our home is gone!' he wailed.
'Where's my family?
What'll I do?'

'Don't worry,' I said. 'They'll come back, I'm sure. I'll find you a place to stay for now near where I live. And they'll find you when they come home. But there's one problem.'

'Yes?' asked Barny.

'Em . . . you'll need to be able to fly.'

'Fly? Me? Now?'

'It's easy,' I told him, hoping he wouldn't ask me to show him.

'Show me,' said Barny.

'Well, you just hop onto a branch, like this, flap your wings, close your eyes – and jump.'

I jumped, and landed with another bump on the hard ground. 'Ouch!' I shouted. This *was* a day for crash landings and sore bottoms!

'Are you all right?' shouted Barny.

'Great!' I said, hoping he would try it next.

Up he climbed. He closed his eyes
and flapped his wings.

'It's just no good. I
can't jump,' he
yelled.

'Open your
eyes,
Barny,' I
shouted
from the
ground.

He did. He
saw that he was
flying through
the air.

'Wheeee! Yipeeee!' he called. Then he stopped flapping and looked down at me. 'This is . . . Oops!' He had started to fall.

'FLAP!' I shouted. And luckily he did. *Barny could fly!*

'This is cool!' he said. 'I feel like a bird.'

'You *are* a bird, dummy,' I said. And owls are supposed to be wise, I thought.

He landed a bit bumpily beside me.

'Come on, I'll give you a lift. It's great up there.' He was so excited and proud.

I wasn't sure. After all, he had only just learned to fly. Was it safe? I didn't want another hard landing.

'Up,' Barny ordered, getting quite cocky now.

Well, in the end I climbed on board.

'Hold on tight,' Barny yelled, 'we'll have some fun.'

And we did. We sailed over fields and trees. We soared high and met a skylark. We flew over cows and rabbits, and dipped low over the river. We went to look down over Malone's farm, and the dogs barked their heads off at us.

'This is exciting,' said Barny.

'Great!' I agreed.

Then we glided over some elm trees where there was a rookery.

The rooks were annoyed and started to chase us. Barny flew hard but we couldn't get away.

Then we saw something hovering in the air.

'What's that?' I asked.

'Don't know,' said Barny. 'Some sort of bird.'

The shape swooped near us and we nearly crashed into it. It was a *very fast* flyer.

'S-s-s-sorry . . .' stuttered Barny.

'What's wrong with you two?' asked the bird.

'Those rooks are chasing us and I only just learned how to fly.'

'Don't worry,' said the bird. 'Follow me.'

He flew across over the fields towards Malone's farmhouse. There he landed just inside the top window of the barn. We followed.

The rooks settled noisily on the roof of the barn, calling at us.

They were joined by two magpies, and they all made such a racket that Mr Malone came out of the house with his shotgun.

'Get out of there,' he yelled and pointed his gun in the air. We heard a loud bang. Then a big black cloud rose in the air and the rooks were off, followed by the magpies.

'That's the worst noise I ever heard,' said Barny.

'That's a gun,' said the bird. 'A sound to fear more than any other.'

Barny looked frightened.

'But *you* don't have to worry,' said the bird. 'Nor do I. I'm a kestrel, you see, and owls and kestrels catch mice and rats, so we keep the farmers happy.'

What about *me*? I wondered. Nobody's said anything about *me*.

'But not all men know we're helpful to farmers,' continued the kestrel. 'So it's always best to be careful.'

Barny nodded. I nodded too, even if they didn't notice.

'You should be safe now,' said the kestrel, and he suddenly took off and flew away as fast as the fastest wind.

Barny gazed after him. 'Great bird,' he said. 'Great flyer.'

'Come on,' I said. 'Let's go!'

And off we went to find a place for him to live.

It was quite dark when we came in over the tree tops of our own wood. Barny made for a beech tree, but he missed and landed instead on top of Farmer Malone, who was out walking his dogs! What bad luck!

'Ouch!' shouted Mr Malone as Barny gripped the top of his head in fright. I hung on tightly to Barny.

'What the blazes is this?' Malone yelled. He couldn't see a thing because Barny's wings were spread over his eyes!

The dogs were barking madly and jumping up trying to get at Barny.

Mr Malone gave a swipe at us with his stick. Then Barny gave his famous loud shriek! Poor Malone got such a fright that he took off like a hare across the fields, his dogs chasing after him.

Barny and I flew on into the woods and he managed to land safely on a tall pine tree. This can be Barny's home for now, I decided, and both of us curled up and fell asleep.

*   *   *

All that was just to tell you about Barny and me and how we became best friends. Now I'm going to tell you about his hoot. Or his non-hoot!

We woke next morning to the sound of the dawn chorus. But there were other sounds too, and when I looked down I saw all my woodland friends below – Renny Fox, Bentley Badger, Harry Hedgehog, Ollie Otter and Billy Blackbird. They had heard about Barny's home.

'Did my family come back?' said Barny in a wobbly voice.

But nobody had seen them.

'They'll come, don't you worry,' said Renny Fox. 'Come on down and have some breakfast!'

We dropped to the ground, and all of us sat around and had a great picnic.

Then we decided to play a few games to cheer up poor Barny who was still a bit down.

Harry Hedgehog rolled himself into a ball and we played Roll Harry. Renny Fox rolled him to me. I rolled him to Bentley Badger. He rolled him to Barny. It was great fun but we had to stop when Harry got too dizzy!

Then Billy Blackbird flew up to his favourite perch and sang two beautiful forest songs. Billy is always a bit serious, but singing is his best thing.

I juggled five nuts without letting any of them fall. Then I ate them!

Renny chased his tail, and we all roared laughing because he looked so silly. Then he told some very bad jokes. We all roared laughing again just to please him.

Bentley scratched a lovely design on a tree trunk.

Ollie did a few somersaults and back flips.

'Come on, Barny,' I shouted at last, 'it's your turn.'

'What'll I do?' he asked.

'Why don't you hoot?' said Billy Blackbird.

'Yes,' I agreed, 'let's hear you hoot. We've only ever heard you give those terrible shrieks.'

We all sat around, waiting while Barny got ready to hoot. He closed his eyes, took a deep breath and . . . hissed!

'That wasn't a hoot,' I said. 'Try again.'

He got ready again. Eyes closed,
Barny tried hard. Out came a snore!

'That's not a hoot either,' said Ollie
Otter.

Barny closed his eyes a third time,
took a huge breath, and then let out the
loudest shriek I have ever heard.

Harry rolled into a ball in fright. Billy
took off into the air. I blocked my ears.

'Aren't you *able* to hoot?' asked Renny.

'I . . . I don't seem to know how,' said poor Barny.

Then I opened my big mouth and said: 'Imagine! An owl who couldn't give a hoot!' Everyone laughed.

Barny flew to the top of the tree and turned his back on us. He was really upset.

Billy, who thinks he knows everything, said: 'You know, it's very serious for an owl not to be able to hoot. Poor Barny!' 'Yes,' agreed Renny. 'When I was a small cub I used to hear the owls in the Pine Forest hooting to each other all the time. I never heard of one who couldn't hoot.'

'I remember them hooting as well,' agreed Ollie.

'This is very serious, indeed,' said Billy seriously. 'He must have lost it.'

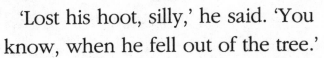

'Lost what?' I asked.

'Lost his hoot, silly,' he said. 'You know, when he fell out of the tree.'

Now, *I* had fallen out of the tree too – maybe I had lost something? I decided to test things, just in case. I ran and jumped. I raced up the tree trunk. I checked my whiskers. Everything seemed to be in place.

Barny was still at the top of the tree. I skipped up to him.

'Come on, Barny,' I said. 'It's not the end of the world.'

'Imagine! An owl who cannot hoot!' he said. 'It's like a hedgehog who can't roll into a ball. Or like a squirrel who couldn't tumble over!'

I had forgotten to test that one. So I did it there and then at the top of the tree. Barny thought I did it for him and he tried to laugh.

'You must have lost your hoot when you fell out of the tree,' I told him.

'Do you think so?' he asked.

'Well, if it's been lost, it can be found,' I announced. 'Come on, everyone,' I shouted down to them all, 'we're going on a hoot hunt.'

'That'll be a hoot,' joked Harry, but
not loud enough for Barny to hear.
We all set out to look for Barny's hoot.

'What does a hoot look like?' said
Renny.
'And what colour is it?' asked Harry.
Barny looked at him blankly.
'How can we look for it when we don't
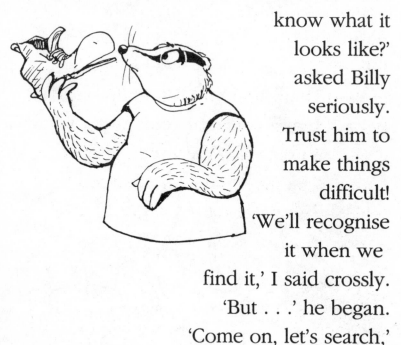
know what it
looks like?'
asked Billy
seriously.
Trust him to
make things
difficult!
'We'll recognise
it when we
find it,' I said crossly.
'But . . .' he began.
'Come on, let's search,'
I said quickly.

We went to the fallen tree where
Barny had lived. All we found was a
pile of logs and a few twigs. Then we
looked all around and found an old
boot, a bottle, a jay's feather, a hat with
a pair of field mice nesting in it, even
some of Bentley's hair on a barbed wire
fence – but no hoot.

Billy didn't search at all. He sat thinking.

'Maybe . . .' he said.

Oh no, I thought, another problem coming up.

'Maybe . . .' he said again. 'You see, none of us ever actually *saw* a hoot. We've only *heard* it. Maybe you can't see it at all!'

'You mean,' said Harry, annoyed, 'we're searching for something you can't see?'

'Exactly,' said Billy.

I had to admit he had a point. 'How can we search for it so?' I asked.

'We can *listen* for it,' said Billy.

'Quiet, everyone,' ordered Renny.

We all sat still, listening. We heard the cows in a distant field mooing. We heard a dog barking in the farmyard. We heard insect noises – I certainly heard a bee buzzing close to my ear!

'Go away!' I said.

'Shush,' said everyone else.

We listened again. Nothing.

'It's no use,' moaned Barny. 'My hoot is gone forever!'

A little painted lady butterfly flew close by. 'Maybe it just blew away?' she suggested.

We hadn't thought of that.

'Well, I've often been blown away by a strong wind, and I *must* be heavier than a hoot,' she said.

I wasn't sure about that. She didn't look all that heavy to me.

'But it could be anywhere, then,' said Bentley. 'It could have blown over the sea.'

'We'll never find it,' said Barny. 'You must all stop looking. You have better things to do.'

But we all agreed to continue.

'Anyway, it's great fun,' said Harry.

The day had almost gone and it was getting dark. Suddenly Billy shouted: 'I know! Maybe a hoot only comes out at night.'

That was pretty smart, I thought, I wish *I'd* thought of that.

'Of course! That's the time for hooting. That's when I always heard them long ago,' said Ollie.

'Brilliant!' I said. 'I'm glad we thought of that.'

'It was *I* who thought of it,' snapped Billy.

We sat down anyway and listened again. All we heard was a woodcock calling to the moon.

Then silence. Then suddenly the sound of twigs breaking . . . and barking.

'What's that?' said Ollie.

'Dogs!' yelled Renny. 'Scatter!'

Two dogs came rushing out of the dark towards us. We ran off in different directions.

I shot straight up the nearest tree.
Billy flew away, making the worst
scolding sound I've ever heard. Harry
curled into a ball and rolled down the
hill. Bentley raced off at a very quick
pace for a badger. Barny flitted around
the tops of the trees like a giant white
moth.

Renny and Ollie headed into the thick undergrowth of the woods and the dogs decided to chase them. They raced off, barking loudly. Soon they had trapped Renny and Ollie in a narrow hole, and they sat outside barking and growling.

Suddenly a long streak of light fell across the ground. It was a man carrying a torch – and a gun!

Oh no, I thought, Renny and Ollie are done for!

He ran up to the dogs, pointed his gun into the hole . . . and just then Barny gave his loudest shriek ever and flew out of a tree above the man's head.

The man got such a fright he spun around and the gun went off into the air. The dogs raced to the tree where Barny had landed. And Renny and Ollie ran out of the hole and off into the woods.

'Come on, Blackie,' called the man. 'Come, Grey. It's only an owl. We're going home.'

There was a long silence after they
left, then, one by one, we all came out.
All except Barny.

'Where's Barny?' asked Renny. 'He's
the hero. He saved our lives.'

But where was he?

We searched around and found him
lying at the bottom of the beech tree.
There was a red stain on his lovely
white feathers.

We stood over him in silence. Harry was the first to reach out and touch him.

'He's alive!' said Harry.

We propped Barny up against the tree trunk. He opened his eyes once, stared at us, then closed them again.

Nobody knew what to do.

A rabbit from a nearby warren came over to see what was going on. 'What's up?' he asked.

We told him about Barny.

'Take him to Old Lepus,' the rabbit said. 'He can cure anything.'

'Who?' we all asked together.

'Old Lepus is the wisest animal in the woods. And he's used to friends being wounded by guns.'

We gathered some sticks to make a stretcher for Barny, then Renny and Bentley carried him, the rabbit showing us the way.

Old Lepus lived in a cedar tree. Ollie knocked on the door.

'Who's that?' asked a cheerful voice. 'Who's coming at this late hour?'

'Our friend Barny's been shot,' called
Renny.

Out came a white-whiskered hare.

'Let me see,' he said. 'Oh dear, oh
dear. You'd better leave him here with
me. If you all just wait outside, I'll see
what I can do.'

We sat outside in silence. I have never
seen so many sad faces.

Then a woodcock flying nearby came
over and said: 'I hear someone's
looking for an owl's hoot.'

The hoot! We had forgotten all about
it.

'I don't think I give a hoot about it
now,' I said. I didn't mean it as a joke,
and anyway, nobody laughed.

'Oh yes, the hoot,' said Renny at last. 'A good friend of ours lost it.'

'Well, I heard lots of hoots near the Pine Forest a short while ago.'

We looked at each other. Should we stay and see that he was going to get better, or should we go and try to find the hoot?

'Well, it would be nice if we could have the hoot for him when he got better,' I said. 'It might cheer him up.'

'It might even help him get better quickly,' said Ollie.

'That's settled, then,' announced Renny, and we all set off, the woodcock flying ahead to show us the way.

At last he called out: 'This is the place. Good luck! I hope you find it!' and away he flew.

'Here we go again,' said Harry. 'Quiet everyone!'

We listened. There was a deep silence for a few minutes and then . . . and then . . . a hoot!

'Listen,' I shouted. 'Did you hear it?'

'Quiet!' they all said.

We heard it again.

'Hoot, hoot, HOOT.' It was getting louder and louder.

'It's coming our way,' said Harry, and he seemed almost afraid. Afraid of a hoot, I ask you!

'HOOT, HOOT, HOOT.'

A brown owl flew over our heads.

'It's only him,' said Ollie, disappointed.

'Whoooos there?' The owl landed on a tree near us.

We explained why we were there and how our friend Barny had lost his hoot.

There were hoots of laughter from the owl. He laughed and hooted so much we thought he was going to be sick!

'What's so funny?' I asked.

'Ho! Ho! Ho! Hoot! Hoot! Ha! Ha! You lot *are* a hoot!'

We weren't too pleased.

'If we were a hoot,' said Harry, 'we wouldn't need to go looking for one!'

'You tell him!' said Billy.

'Your friend could blow and wheeze until he was blue in the face,' explained the brown owl, 'and he would *never* hoot!'

'Never?' said Ollie.

'Well, I can see you don't give a hoot about him!' snapped Renny.

'And we don't give a hoot about you,' added Harry boldly, and he started to walk away.

'Oh sorry! Sorry!' said the owl. 'I must explain. You see, your friend Barny is a *barn owl* and they *never* hoot!'

'Never?' we all said together.

'Never,' he said again. 'I am a *long-eared owl* and hooting comes naturally to me and to my cousins the *tawny owls*. But barn owls have never, never been known to hoot. *Never.*'

'Never!' said Harry again. 'I think we've got the point,' I snapped.

'This is terrible,' said Renny. 'Poor Barny was so looking forward to hooting.'

'And it's all my fault,' I said. 'I started all this by asking him to hoot in the first place.'

'No! It was me actually,' sighed Billy.

'Well, who's going to tell him?' I asked, hoping they wouldn't say me.

'You should,' said Billy and they all nodded. 'You were his first friend.'

'I don't know what all this fuss is about,' said the brown owl. 'There's nothing special about hooting. *I* wish I could sing like a blackbird, but I can't. In fact, Barny makes a much more impressive sound. Something like this . . . '

He made a sound that was something like a sneeze.

'I never heard Barny do *that!*' I said.

He tried again. This time the noise he made sounded like a cat in pain.

'No! Not that either!' I said.

'Well, I'm afraid I simply can't make that wonderful shriek.'

'Shriek!' I shrieked. 'You mean *that's* his special sound?'

'Well, I have to say,' said Renny, 'Barny's shriek *is* much more interesting than a hoot any day, or night! No offence meant,' he said to the brown owl.

'And if Barny hadn't shrieked when he did, the man with the gun would have got Renny and me!' said Ollie. 'I don't think a hoot could do that!'

We all agreed.

'Well,' said the brown owl, 'I suggest you go right now and tell him to forget all this nonsense about not being able to hoot. I'll come and explain! By the way, my name is Otus.'

'Thanks for coming with us,' said Harry. 'I'm glad you *do* give a hoot about Barny.'

'Oh I do,' said Otus. 'In fact I give two hoots about him.'

We all laughed loudly.

Then we hurried back to Old Lepus's place. There we found Barny chatting happily to Lepus.

'I'm fine,' he said. 'It was just a small wound.'

'We have something to tell you,' Billy said seriously.

Otus explained to Barny that he must not worry about hooting, that barn owls are not hooters. And that his shriek was just as good – if not better!

'Silly me,' I added, 'asking you to hoot in the first place.'

'No, it was me,' said Billy.

'We're *all* to blame,' said Renny finally.

'But thank you all for going to such trouble for me,' said Barny. 'You're all true friends.'

'I think it's time for supper,' announced Old Lepus, and he invited us all to stay.

'Quiet,' yelled Harry suddenly, at the top of his voice..

What *now*! I wondered.

'I thought I heard something,' he said.

Then we all heard it. A few faint shrieks!

'Shrieks!' said Barny excitedly. 'Owls! Barn owls! Maybe . . .'

It *was*. His parents and brothers and sister flew down.

'Found you at last!' shrieked Barny's mother, and the whole family gathered around him, shrieking.

'We have been searching everywhere for you,' said his father.

'And *we've* been everywhere searching for his hoot!' said Harry, unfortunately.

'What hoot?' asked Barny's mother.

'Well, it's sort of hard to explain,' I began . . .

'It's sort of *awkward* to explain,' began Renny . . .

'*Silly*, more like,' said Ollie . . .

'Let's all have supper before the food gets cold,' interrupted Old Lepus.

And we did.

*　*　*

So that's the story of me putting my foot in my mouth!

And now, let me remind you – if you're ever out at night, listen very carefully and you too may hear the famous shriek of the owl who couldn't give a hoot!

OTHER BOOKS FROM THE O'BRIEN PRESS

From Don Conroy:

THE TIGER WHO WAS A ROARING SUCCESS
A strange visitor turns up in the woodlands.

CARTOON FUN
How to draw your own cartoons – people, faces, animals,
monsters, dinosaurs . . . and more

ON SILENT WINGS
The story of a little owl who must survive on his own in a
world full of danger.

Watch out for:

WILDLIFE FUN
How to draw animals, both realistic and cartoon. Also
details and facts about the animals you're drawing.

* * *

THE LOUGH NEAGH MONSTER
Sam McBratney
Illustrated by Donald Teskey
You've heard of the Loch Ness monster? Well, here she
visits her quiet Irish cousin! A hilarious story set in the
North of Ireland.

LOOK! LOOK! THE GIGGLE BOOK
William Cole
Illustrated by Tomi Ungerer
A bookful of laughs and fun and silliness, with great
drawings.